What Was Communism?
A SERIES EDITED BY TARIQ ALI

The theory of Communism as enunciated by Marx and Engels in *The Communist Manifesto* spoke the language of freedom, allied to reason. A freedom from exploitation in conditions that were being created by the dynamic expansion of capitalism so that 'all that is solid melts into air'. The system was creating its own grave-diggers. But capitalism survived. It was the regimes claiming loyalty to the teachings of Marx that collapsed and reinvented themselves. What went wrong?

This series of books explores the practice of twentieth-century Communism. Was the collapse inevitable? What actually happened in different parts of the world? And is there anything from that experience that can or should be rehabilitated? Why have so many heaven-stormers become submissive and gone over to the camp of reaction? With capitalism mired in a deep crisis, these questions become relevant once again. Marx's philosophy began to be regarded as a finely spun web of abstract and lofty arguments, but one that had failed the test of experience. Perhaps, some argued, it would have been better if his followers had remained idle dreamers and refrained from political activity. The Communist system lasted 70 years and failed only once. Capitalism has existed for over half a millennium and failed regularly. Why is one collapse considered the final and the other episodic? These are some of the questions explored in a variety of ways by writers from all over the globe, many living in countries that once considered themselves Communist states.

two underdogs and a cat

three reflections on communism

SLAVENKA DRAKULIC

LONDON NEW YORK CALCUTTA

Seagull Books 2009

© Slavenka Drakulic 2009

ISBN-13   978 1 9064 9 728 6

British Library Cataloguing-in-Publication Data
A catalogue record for this book is available
from the British Library

Jacket and book designed by Sunandini Banerjee, Seagull Books
Printed at Rockwel Offset, Calcutta

*In memory
of my long-gone
canine friends, Kiki and Charlie*

Contents

ix
Acknowledgements

1
A Guided Tour
through the Museum of Communism

39
An Interview
with the Oldest Dog in Bucharest

73
The Cat-Keeper in Warsaw
(A Letter to the Prosecutor)

Acknowledgements

I would like to thank friends in the Fischer Foundation in Germany for their generous grant which enabled me to work on this book. My thanks to the IWM, the Institute for Human Sciences, in Vienna, and to their anonymous friend who financed my Milena Jesenska grant in 2008.

I am grateful to Rujana for her inspiration, to Andi for his enthusiasm and to Richard for his improvements—as well as to my friends for their trust and support.

Who controls the past controls the future.
Who controls the present controls the past.

George Orwell

I

A Guided Tour
through the Museum of Communism

Come in, come in, please! Don't worry, this is only a *museum* of Communism—not the real thing!

I'm joking. But do come in, please. You are Hans, from Würzburg, I presume? I was expecting you. I am Bohumil, your distant relative. I live here

SLAVENKA DRAKULIC

in a school cabinet, among the old textbooks. It suits me. I'm a bookish type, a book-mouse, one could say—ha-ha! Some time ago, my grammar school became a private university. The classrooms were refurbished and my cabinet was thrown out. I thought that was the end of my comfortable life. Luckily, some people from the Museum came along and brought the cabinet here, as an exhibit from the old times.

I share my days with Milena, an elderly cleaning woman who also sells souvenirs in the Museum shop. She pretends she doesn't know I live here. But why, then, I ask you, did she try to kill me with her broom the very first time she saw me—an ordinary little mouse? Well, not kill perhaps but scare me off.

As I had no other place to go, she reconciled herself to my existence. Perhaps she thinks I am an underdog too? Now she leaves crumbs of bread and bits of apple and cheese near my cabinet every evening before she leaves. Often, when we are alone, she acts as if she is talking to herself but we both know that she is talking to me. She calls me Bohumil! She says, '*Do you know, Bohumil, what happened to me*

A GUIDED LIFE

today?'—and then goes on with her story. I usually stand on the window sill and listen to her, keep her company. It took me some time to understand that, since there is nobody around, Bohumil is—well, me!

She's stepped out for a cigarette—she won't be back for a while. The only thing I hold against Milena is that she's a heavy smoker, even though it's bad for her health. And for mine. In fact, I discovered I'm allergic to cigarettes. Although she does often open the window into the courtyard to let out the bad air. It's an old habit from when she used to work in the state archive as a secretary. Not as a cleaner, mind you. Milena studied English and French. Speaking of air, she says that any institution that has anything to do with the Communist state, even this one, smells of dust. Perhaps from too many papers, documents about God-knows-what and God-knows-whom . . . Milena used to worry, you know, about whether her husband was registered in the files of the secret police. Of course he was! Like he was a 'security risk'! '*Any state that has to depend on police reports about citizens like him, just an ordinary engineer*

SLAVENKA DRAKULIC

in an electrical plant, is pathetic!' she used to say to her friend Dasha, a cleaning woman from the casino downstairs. But, obviously, that's how it was. Every citizen was a 'security risk' back then. However, in the new democracy, because of so-called *privatization*, her Marek lost his job. That's why she works here. They need the money.

I can't say I mind living in here, in the Museum, although life was much more interesting in the grammar school. I learned a lot about Communism from the lectures of a history teacher. Perlik was his name. I'd heard he was also a poet, a kind of dissident intellectual, and that he even spent some time in jail when he was young.

You don't have such a museum in Würzburg, you say, and your knowledge of Communism is non-existent? Well, since you're here in Prague as a tourist, I could show you around. I consider myself qualified to be a guide here, but the sad truth is that the Museum will not employ a mouse. I can tell you that the more time I spend here, the more I realize how important the Museum is. I remember Professor Perlik's words: '*A time will soon come when kids will ask,* "*Communism, what*'s *that? A religion? Maybe a car manufacturer?*" ' And from the things I heard him say, that's simply not right. Communism shouldn't be remembered just by the likes of the Professor, or Milena who survived it—it should be remembered for its bad sides and its good. There must be something good one can say about it, although that's not a popular view to hold these days, I gather. For example, people could get a solid education, they say. Or there's the fact that Communist USSR fought against the Nazis in the Second World War. Yet Milena says that, after watching Hollywood movies, one gets the impression that it was the Americans who won it all on their own!

No, life under Communism should not be forgotten, although that is exactly what I see happening. In the Museum shop, by the way, you can buy a history book about the dark past for only five euros. It's cheap. And it's only a hundred pages long, in large print. '*The older I get, the more I appreciate it,*' says Milena. You can read there, for example (I heard

SLAVENKA DRAKULIC

someone reading it with my own ears!), that the wife of President Klement Gottwald was rather fat, or that the wife of Antonin Novotny (the man who later became President) took the china and the bedsheets from the flat of Vladimir Clementis. Of course, only after he was executed in the purges of the Fifties. You can also learn—as I did—that two hundred and fifty-seven thousand and nine hundred and sixty-four people sentenced for political reasons were rehabilitated in 1990.

Some visitors don't care at all about such facts. They just buy posters, stamps, T-shirts and Soviet army caps, along with candles shaped like Stalin, Marx and Lenin. They are the most popular items sold in the shop. Maybe because they are the cheapest. I admit I can hardly imagine the excitement of watching Stalin slowly melt into a puddle of wax, but there are people who enjoy such symbolic acts.

As you come in, you inevitably notice the busts and statues of Marx, Lenin, Stalin. A young man, a Czech, was here recently. Looking at Marx, he said:

A GUIDED TOUR

'*Is that some Orthodox priest?*' I suppose Marx, with his beard, does indeed look like one. You could also say that he was rather orthodox in his views, and, in some ways, quite like a priest, preaching his doctrine. But even I was astonished by the young man's ignorance. What would Professor Perlik have made of his question? He would wonder what they teach in history class nowadays and would probably tell the boy: '*Well, read about him, you* durak!' That's 'stupid' in Russian, which he also taught, but they don't teach anybody Russian any more. Sad, but true. From my limited perspective, a language is a language. It is worth learning regardless of the historical circumstances—no? But what can such an ignorant person read here in the Museum about a historical figure like Karl Marx and the origins of Communism? See, here it says he was '*a bohemian and an intellectual adventurer, who started his career as a romantic poet with an inclination towards apocalyptic titanism, a sharp-tongued journalist*'—as if that would somehow disqualify him from writing *Das Kapital*?! Or, look at this text about Lenin: '*From the very beginning, Lenin pushed for the tactics*

[1]

of extreme perfidiousness and ruthlessness which became characteristic of all communist regimes of the time.' What can I tell you? I know from Professor Perlik's lectures that, in Communist times, Lenin was glorified much too much. And that textbooks were even more laced with such descriptions and such cheap psychology! But the Professor would probably say that there is no need for ideology nowadays, we need history instead.

You know, sometimes, when visitors come to this room with its paintings from the Soviet school of socialist realism, with the busts and a space shuttle and a school class and a workshop—all in one room!—I can see how disappointed they are. I peek out at them and they look to me like those people who love to visit freak shows with two-headed goats or bearded women. Of course, I can see why they are disappointed—there is no Stalin in a cage, not even a mummy of Lenin! Only a heap of old things here, more like a junkyard, which in fact it is. The exhibits here are from flea markets, all kinds of garage sales, even out of dustbins. See, here Com-

A GUIDED TOUR

munism is finally reduced to the rubbish dump of history! Isn't that what the Velvet Revolution of 1989 was all about? That is what I'd like to tell them when I see them turning up their noses and thinking: '*Is that* all *you have here*?' What more would they want to *see*?

Permit me to say that, from what I have heard from the Professor, Communism is not so much about exhibits, about *seeing*, but more about how one lived in those times, or, more to the point, how one survived them. From the lack of food or shoes to the lack of freedom and human rights. The question is, how do you present that kind of shortage, shortages that were not just poverty-induced, to somebody who knows very little about it? Because people who experienced life under Communism tend not to come here anyway . . . I am afraid that our Innocent Visitors, as I call such people, have to use their imaginations. I sometimes think that Milena is the Museum's best 'exhibit'—she's lived most of her life under Communism. If only visitors would ask her about her life . . . but nobody does.

★ SLAVENKA DRAKULIC

Let me first tell you about the Museum itself, advertised as 'above McDonald's, next to the Casino'. Indeed, it is very properly situated in Na Prikope Street, *'in the heart of consumer capitalism'*, as one visitor remarked the other day. It was opened in December 2001 in the nineteenth-century Palais Savarin. It stores roughly one thousand artefacts in four rooms and was founded privately by an American of Czech origin. Why was it privately funded? Excellent question, Hans, and very logical too! Because, astonishingly enough, nobody from the democratic government hit upon this idea. Strange, you may think, that such an important era of the recent past would not have been documented had it not been for a couple of enthusiasts. You think that is because it deals with too painful a time, that the memories are still too vivid? Well, I wonder about that. If you ask Milena, there's another reason why the Czechs (or the Slovaks, for that matter. This is their museum, too!) don't care about such a museum and don't visit it either: *'They want to run as far away from Communism as they can. Our young people don't care.*

A GUIDED TOUR

Communism is the ancient past to them. Those old enough to remember now want to forget. And why? Because they had gone along with it. As had I. As had my husband, and our neighbours and everybody we knew, every Pavel and Jelena around us.'

I once heard Professor Perlik say that, today, everybody claims they weren't members of the Communist Party. That they didn't really belong. '*If you believed what people say, you'd think not a single person in this whole country was ever a member of the Communist Party of Czechoslovakia! That they all were victims! That's stupid, given the fact that ten per cent of the population were Party members, plain and simple. That means one million and seven hundred thousand people! I understand that not all of them were believers, that they were only formal members because of the jobs and careers and benefits that came with membership. But no regime, however totalitarian, could exist without complicity on the part of the people—however unwilling it might be. Let's not fool ourselves. Most of us complied not only in order to survive—because Czechoslovakia was not the USSR—but to live better. I admit it's a hard fact to face now. But yes, there is a difference between those who were members only formally and those who really collaborated.*

⭐ SLAVENKA DRAKULIC

Perhaps it sounds to you as if there isn't? Collaboration is a more active attitude, a kind of partnership. For example, while ordinary citizens merely complied, members of the Party collaborated with the regime. There are many shades of grey.'

I realized that it is not without reason that the history of the Communist Party of Czechoslovakia is written on a single scroll and, glued to the wall, almost as if it is not intended to be read. I guess what I'm trying to explain is that I learned how the most important things about Communism are the invisible ones. And that, in here, in the Museum, you won't see *the shades of grey* that prevailed in everyday life. That is why such a museum *reaches only so deep*— this criticism comes from a very learned man who was here, perhaps a curator in another museum, perhaps some kind of critic. According to him, the Museum does not—and cannot—show you the full depth of what the people endured. '*There is no personal history given here, no individual destiny*,' he said. On the other hand, perhaps no museum of Communism is capable of doing that. And you know what I think? Not that the opinion of someone like me

A GUIDED TOUR

counts at all, nevertheless I tell you that maybe the Museum's got it right! Maybe the absence of individual stories is the best illustration of the fact that individualism was the biggest sin one could commit.

But I'm getting too pedagogical, I'm afraid! My dear Hans, you must tell me if I'm treating you like a total ignoramus, you must stop me if I'm boring you! I guess my attitude stems from the fact that too many Americans pass through the Museum nowadays . . .

But you'd like me to go on? OK then, where was I? Yes, I wanted to say that Communist regimes generally seemed to prefer numbers over stories. Numbers are abstract, they create a kind of 'scientific' neutrality. Let me give you one of Professor Perlik's examples. I've heard him tell his history class that Hitler exterminated about six million Jews in Europe during the Second World War. His students looked at him blankly, then continued chatting and pushing and throwing things at each other. The information didn't even catch their attention, let alone their imaginations. But then he took them to Poland.

SLAVENKA DRAKULIC

To Auschwitz. I remember them talking afterwards about that visit, about how memorable that spring day had been for them. Of course, Professor Perlik had already told them what had happened there, but they were totally unprepared. Evidently, nothing can prepare you for such a horror—'*And that is a good thing*,' he'd said. '*You grasp the horror better once you see, with your own eyes, the heaps of human hair, shoes, glasses . . . Heaps. All those things, every item, belonged to an individual with a name, to a real live person.*' He also told them that, during Communism, he would not have been able to share with them the fact that about thirty million people died in the labour camps in Siberia—the subject was taboo. But I suspect he had anyway—and so landed up in prison.

Now, let's get back to what you actually see here. Only a pile of dusty things. Like an antique shop or a flea market somewhere in Kosice (I've never been there, but I've heard someone making the comparison). Therefore, it seems more important to see the invisible yet omnipresent ugliness of

A GUIDED TOUR

the Communist mentality, of which the artefacts in the Museum are just a reflection. By mentality, I mean a certain way of thinking and behaving that developed over decades and under harsh conditions. Not solidarity, as you might expect of people living under duress, but its opposite—selfishness, *a slow hardening of the soul* (this formulation, you rightly guess, comes from the more poetic side of our Professor). Yet, only art, especially literature, can show you that. Novels like those of a certain Milan Kundera, a writer whose name I have often heard mentioned of late.

Our visitors usually want to take photos in this room. For example, if they stand here, where I am standing, they can take a photo of this beautiful nineteenth-century chandelier. Indeed, they can get it in the same frame as the hammer and sickle—a really nice souvenir! By the way, this chandelier is widely considered by our visitors to be the Museum's only beautiful item. Although not intended as an exhibit, you could still say—as I have heard them say—that it symbolizes the life of the bourgeoisie, the class enemy. As does this whole spacious apartment. '*Look, a beautiful bourgeois apartment full of ugly things produced during Communism!*'

I seem to like the fact that this is a museum of ugly things. By the time visitors like you arrive here, they have had their fill of beautiful buildings in the neighbourhood. So they don't notice beauty any longer. Golden altars, baroque facades, angels, Madonnas, spectacular church paintings . . . Indeed, I have seen such things myself during my excursions to the neighbourhood. Here, in the Museum, as in real Communism, ugliness reigns. Sometimes I hear foreigners wonder aloud why Communism doesn't care about beauty. You only need to go to the southern outskirts of Prague to see whole blocks of ghastly grey dorms—*panelak*s, built out of prefabricated material in the Seventies. (By the way, that stuff's great for us mice—so easy to make a nice home there!) Yet these buildings provided a home for millions of people (and mice)—for the so-called proletariat!—who moved from their villages to the

A GUIDED TOUR

city to work in the industries. Milena and her Marek still live in such a building, in a sixty-three square metre, two-room apartment. They were happy when they got it in the Sixties, after years of waiting in a single rented room heated only by a coal stove.

Almost anything produced under Communism anywhere—from apartment buildings to clothes, from furniture to pots and pans—is considered ugly. Although this was less the case in this very country, where the Communist system was originally built by and for poor peasants—where would they get a sense of beauty? Functionality, not looks, was the priority in every aspect, the arts included. Hence, socialist realism, of course. Any divergence from that rule—abstract painting, for example—was forbidden, even punished, as in the USSR after the Thirties. Art in general—painting, for instance—had a political–ideological–educational role, much as did those mediaeval frescos that explained the beginning of the world (and religion) to the masses. Ugliness was built into that system—that's what I learned from Jana Strugalova, who taught art in our grammar school and who was herself very beautiful. Some examples you see exhibited here, like the furniture in this 'typical living room'. 'Lifestyle!' it says. As if poverty were a 'style'! Style is something one chooses—even a mouse knows that . . .

Now, if you take a look at the representation of a typical school classroom to your right, what do you see? A blackboard, a few benches and a cabinet—that's where I live, by the way. It doesn't tell you much, except perhaps for one detail. Have you noticed that the writing in the textbooks and on the blackboard are in the Cyrillic alphabet? No? The Czech alphabet uses the Latin script. This exhibit obviously symbolizes a Soviet classroom. You must have also noticed that most of the objects exhibited so far have to do with the Soviet Union, not Czechoslovakia, as the country was called before the split in 1993. If you pay attention to the details, it is easy to conclude that the USSR is over-represented in the Museum, as one visitor observed. We are in Prague, after all, but all that visitors get (as you yourself can see) is a kind of written chronology of the

A GUIDED TOUR

Czechoslovak Communist Party in that corridor that you passed. This clearly suggests that Czechs see themselves as the victims of Communism, not as the 'original sinners', so to speak. Later, when we come to 1968, you will see that the rebellion against the Soviet occupation is much better documented. The rebellion is important, something to be proud of, therefore there are a lot of photos, even documentary films. As if the creators of the Museum (but we're not supposed to bite the hand that feeds us, as Milena would say!) were a bit ashamed of Czech history. Of the fact that, say, in the elections of 1946, about forty per cent of the people voted for the Communists. You'll agree that the Czechs can't blame the USSR for that!

Milena says that her family, like millions of others, was guilty of accepting the new political system. Hers is by no means an exceptional story—nobody was jailed, murdered or tortured. Her parents came here after the war from some Bohemian village and got a job in a furniture factory, happy to put their hard life on the land behind them. She and her brother (I saw him when he came to visit her) went to a grammar school. Their parents insisted that they study—that was the only way to a better life, they believed. They were right. The brother became a doctor. Milena studied foreign languages. Soon after, she met her husband. He was a student of electrical engineering. When the baby came, someone had to work and that someone was Milena. They both tried to stay out of politics, accepting Party membership because it was the obvious way to get an apartment, a car, a vacation in Bulgaria. In hindsight, she admits they were passive, meek and submissive. A bit like us mice, you know . . . It was the only way if you were not prepared to go to jail. We would like to forget that now.

Let's stop at this exhibit—a typical shop in the USSR. Shops here looked much better, or so I've been told. Compared to Moscow, the Prague shops were like elegant supermarkets, full of food, especially after 1968, in the period of so-called normalization. Here, we only had two kinds of canned food. That's perhaps an exaggeration—there must

A GUIDED TOUR

have been a few more items in the shops in the USSR, at least in the big cities. Still, you have to imagine what it was like to live on very meagre means. *Ordinary* poverty, you think? I've heard others say so—after all, there was poverty in the West too, especially after the war. Well, you could call it poverty, I suppose, but it wasn't really the same. '*Poverty is when there are things to buy but you don't have the money for them. A shortage is something else—it's when you have the money but there's nothing to buy. The articles are either not produced or not delivered to the shops—because of the way the planned economy works.*' Again, this is how Professor Perlik explained it to his pupils. I mean, you had to be very skilful to get hold of certain products. Shoes, for example. It worked almost like barter, the natural exchange of goods. And if not goods, then services: '*If you give me the medicine I need, I'll help you get a better coat,*' and so on, the Professor explained.

Also, shortages seem to be the key to understanding the end of Communism. You think it was Pope John Paul II? Or Mikhail Gorbachev's idea of *glasnost* and *perestroika*? Or both, combined? Yes, of course, everybody agrees on that. But take a look at this shop again. Toilet paper is not exhibited here, and for good reason: there wasn't any. Nor sanitary towels or diapers or washing powder—not to mention coffee, butter, oranges. Milena remembers that when a friend would travel abroad—Yugoslavia was abroad then because it was outside the Soviet bloc—she would come back with her suitcase full of rolls and rolls of toilet paper! Banalities you might say—but they too decided the destiny of the Communist regime. In order to understand why Communism failed, one has to know that it could not produce the basic things people needed. Or perhaps not enough of them. How long could such regimes last? The success of a political system is also measured in terms of the goods available to ordinary people, I suppose. And to mice, I might add. Sometimes, when I'm making my bed from the fine, soft Italian toilet paper that Milena puts in our toilets, I wonder if my life would have been different if I had been born under Communism.

A GUIDED TOUR ★

Now we come to an interrogation room. Everybody says that this is the Museum's centrepiece. Indeed, here you can see what I mean when I say that much in the Museum is left to the individual imagination. Again, there is not much for you to actually see: a desk, a chair on either side, a lamp, an old typewriter, a hanger from which hangs the notorious black leather coat. Why notorious? Because they say that agents of the Soviet secret police would come for you in the middle of the night wearing just such a coat. Yet what can these *things*, this setting, tell visitors like you, if you don't know what happened in such interrogation rooms? Not much. You can see the statistics on the wall—names and numbers, again. They hide horrible stories, but, as in the case of Auschwitz, these are abstractions. How can one present the people, the living persons, behind the numbers? You have to make an effort to see the individual destiny, a man who has been interrogated and whose spirit is broken. Professor Perlik mentioned Arthur Koestler's book *Darkness at Noon* and Arthur London's *The Confession*, if I remember

SLAVENKA DRAKULIC

correctly. I know that the Professor had a neighbour who testified at the trial of Rudolf Slansky during the first wave of Stalinist purges in the Fifties. He survived the whole ordeal. '*But that man,*' said the Professor, nodding sadly, '*was never the same again.*'

If anything, this room is the symbol of absolute power. In such rooms, people were forced to betray not only others but also themselves. On the other hand, this was the fate of a relative few. But think of something else, not represented here. Think of how the people lived—hundreds of millions of them—with the feeling that an interrogation room had been installed in their brains. You couldn't see it, but it was there. Now, again, you may think that I am exaggerating. But I'm merely speaking of *self-censorship*. A situation in which you become your own interrogator—the very opposite of freedom of expression. What, you wonder, if this was a form of political correctness? My dear Hans, let me put it this way, if I may quote the Professor again: '*Political correctness grew out of a concern for others—self-censorship grew out of a fear of others.*' Mutual surveillance was installed as a

A GUIDED TRUR

system—perfected in the USSR, but practised everywhere. For example, you had no way of knowing if your elderly neighbour, who would even cook you some soup when you were ill, was in fact reporting on your every word and move. If you couldn't trust the people around you, in your house or at work, you would behave cautiously, controlling yourself. The system of surveillance and self-control lives off fear and suspicion. It is a simple and efficient psychological mechanism that turns people into liars, and therefore accomplices of the regime.

But, again, there were *shades of grey* even within this self-censorship. Antonin Novotny was not exactly Stalin, even if there are those who would like to see him like that nowadays. He used to blow his top over films like *Closely Observed Trains* by Jiri Menzel, awarded an Oscar in 1967, and *The Firemen's Ball* by Milos Forman. Or over novels by Ludvik Vaculik, Pavel Kohout and Milan Kundera, all critical of Communism. In the mid-Sixties the atmosphere in this country became so liberal that the new Communist Party Secretary-General, Alexander Dubcek, believed it was even possible to reform Communism when he took up the post in 1967. The invasion by the Warsaw Pact military force in 1968 started because of the Soviet fear of our reforms—of losing their grip on us, that is.

I recently overheard Milena telling some visitors a story. *'That summer, I saw Soviet tanks rolling into the streets of Prague. I will never forget that day. I was barely twenty years old and I'd gone out with my brother. We were running some errands downtown, and he asked me to buy him an ice cream. It was August 21st, a pleasant sunny morning. We were somewhere near the National Theatre, and there, at the corner, was an ice-cream stand. And just as we were turning towards it, we heard a strange noise. Like a thunderstorm at first, then like a huge powerful machine. Indeed, I felt the asphalt tremble under my feet. As we were about to cross the road, we saw a tank at the bottom of the street, about a hundred metres away. A tank in the middle of Prague! I had never seen a real one before—only in war movies. It was slowly coming towards us, very slowly, as if the soldiers were in no particular hurry. I remember we just stood there, staring, hypnotized . . .*

A RUDE GUIDE ★

Here, you see this photo? It was taken on the morning of 21 August 1968 by the Hajny brothers, Jan and Bohumil. Their photos became famous later. You see that woman with the small boy? Well, that happens to be me. Do you notice something odd about this photo? See how the people are behaving? See the woman with the white handbag? She must have heard the tank, she must have seen it coming. But she's walking down the street as if she's taking a stroll, and perhaps deliberately so. Nobody seems to be panicking in this picture and that, considering the tank that's rolling closer and closer, is very strange behaviour—no? You'd think that people would be screaming, running away. But no, the citizens of Prague are slowly walking along, minding their own business, while the occupation army is entering their city. Oh, I just love this photo! No, not because I am in it, but because it captures a certain attitude of the people. Pride, arrogance even, in the face of armed might—like a kind of highly civilized act of protest. Heroism the Czech way. As if we were saying, "We are superior to your tanks." That is how we were—proud, brave. Those tanks did not humiliate us. We felt undefeated, at least for a short while. The best of Czechoslovakia is here in these photos. When you think that it was not about a revolution,

SLAVENKA DRAKULIC

not a demand to abolish Communism, but only to reform it into "socialism with a human face". That day we listened to radio reports about what was happening, about clashes with the tanks in Vinohradska Street. The people of Prague were fighting the Warsaw Pact's seven hundred and fifty thousand troops and six thousand tanks with Molotov cocktails and barricades! We had no chance. Dubcek was kidnapped by the KGB and forced to sign the Moscow Protocol that legalized the Soviet occupation. I still remember that feeling of powerlessness and defeat that settled in and stayed with us for the next twenty years.'

'At least people now know that 1968 in Czechoslovakia was the beginning of the end,' the Professor used to say. *'They learned the hard way that Communism is not to be reformed. But never in their wildest dreams could they have imagined that another attempt to reform Communism—a copy of 1968!—would come from within the USSR itself, and that it would mean its demise. Did you know that Gorbachev was friends with Zdenek Mlynar, one of the leading figures of the Prague Spring? Ah, Gorby, hated and forgotten in his own country . . . I remember how the whole Western world*

A GUIDED TOUR ★

applauded him, as if he really wanted to dispatch Communism to the "graveyard of history", as it were. His achievement was that he did not, could not, send the army against us again (or against other Communist countries, for that matter). And this made it possible for our revolution to be velvet. Not so velvet as one might think, though. My son, a student then, got hit on the head by the police during the November 17th student protest. My daughter soon became a member of the Obcanske Forum and knew Vaclav Havel personally. I remember it all, as if it happened yesterday

. . . Yet, it was twenty years ago when I was standing under the balcony at Vaclavske namesti, *where Havel was speaking, and chanting: "Havel to the castle!" We wanted him to become President and imagine—he did! He did! But once the dream was fulfilled, reality sank in.'*

Here, in the Museum, we have a cinema, where you could, if you had the time, watch documentary films about the revolution. The Velvet Revolution is a well-documented event—even you have heard of it. This perhaps is the reason why not that many visitors sit here and watch—they have already seen it some-

[29]

where. And here, in this cinema, is the end of the story about Communism. In the Museum, I mean.

'*What did the change bring me?*' Milena says. '*I've lost my job. I have less money. My husband drinks. Freedom? What freedom? We can't travel anywhere, we can't buy things. We don't even have a car now, can't afford to keep it,*' she laments to Dasha, who can only share her feelings. I sometimes feel sorry for them, they are obviously among the losers. These two ladies are perhaps not the best advertisement for democracy and capitalism, I'd say. The change happened too late for them. Indeed, how frustrating it must be to finally live in an age of plenty but not be able to enjoy it, don't you think, Hans?

It seems to me, judging from the little knowledge I have managed to acquire from my stay here, in the Museum, that this frustration might be the reason why something mean and suspicious, something hypocritical, still lingers within the people. Traces of former times, I suppose. As if people haven't changed *that* much, not in their minds. I'll give you an example. Milan Kundera whom I mentioned earlier. He's apparently the most famous Czech writer. You may even have seen a film made in Hollywood adapted from his novel, *The Unbearable Lightness of Being*? You know him? Well, then, you also know that all his early novels deal with Communist repression in his country, like *The Joke*. A guy ends up in a labour camp, in a mine, just because a friend wrote him a funny card. Kundera left Czechoslovakia and went to France after the invasion in 1968. He never returned. He became one of the best-known dissidents from the Communist world, next to Alexander Solzhenitsyn.

Suddenly, this same Kundera is in the middle of a scandal! I heard about it from a couple discussing it very loudly in this room just a few days ago. In fact, they woke me up in the middle of my afternoon nap. What happened? In October 2008, a certain historian finds a document—alleged proof that Kundera is not what he seems to be. Not a moral man, but a *denouncer* no less. A document from

1950 is there to prove it. It is a police report, a short one. Stating that Milan Kundera, then a student at the FAMU film academy and an ardent member of the Communist Party, reported to the undersigned police inspector that there was a suspicious person staying in his dormitory. Following this, the police arrested Miroslav Dvoraček, a pilot and a spy for the American-supported Czech intelligence agency. Dvoraček had illegally crossed the border back into Czechoslovakia and was on his way out again. Following Kundera's report, the man was arrested and sentenced to twenty-two years of hard labour. Dvoraček served his sentence mostly in uranium mines. Yet, in his writing and interviews, Kundera never mentions this episode.

'It's the resurrection of that old pattern of suspicion— that nobody is what he claims to be,' I heard the woman say angrily, as if she had personally suffered the consequence of his betrayal. *'A dissident is not a dissident but a fugitive from his not very honourable past. A moral person is, in fact, immoral. Falsehood is truth, and so on. Until yesterday you'd have believed that Kundera was a symbol of morality.'*

A GUIDED TOUR ★

'*Well,*' the man said, rather calmly, '*every normal person should ask himself: but is that report real and not a set-up? How come the document was discovered only now and by what "coincidence"? No one believes in coincidences—there were too many of them in the past. Moreover, what's the purpose of this "discovery" and its publication? In short—who benefits from it today? I tend to just dismiss such coincidences. We should know better. No, the problem lies elsewhere. You see, true or not, the real problem is that this whole devilish story is believable. Convincing. Everybody agrees it could have happened. It could have been that Kundera thought reporting on Dvoraček to be his patriotic duty. He was a Party member, he was in danger of going to prison if he didn't report it. Such were the times. It could have happened to anyone—or so the argument goes.*'

'*But* this *is the false argument!*' the woman interrupted him. '*Kundera is in no way "one of us"! Kundera is—well, Kundera. What about his confession, then? People say, "Why doesn't he confess now, when his big secret is out? He should get it off his chest." Nonsense! They speak such nonsense because, if such a great writer and dissident had made such a terrible denunciation, then our own denunciations and*

★ SLAVENKA DRAKULIC

compromises look comparatively much pettier. So what if Svoboda spied on Markus and he was transferred to a lower-paid job? At least he didn't wind up in prison.'

'*I agree,*' the man said. Now his voice sounded sad. '*There is a certain malevolent triumph in the "fact" (or* the fact, *depending on how you look at it) that the best of us could have each failed. Even if it is not true, even if it is only a suspicion, only a possibility—it excites people. It makes heroes more human, more petty, like the rest of us. If he would only confess, they would immediately grant him forgiveness!*'

'*Ah, yes, forgiveness!—my foot!*' the woman replied, getting even more worked up. '*They couldn't wait to take away his moral credibility—since they couldn't take away his talent and his fame. But he's a stubborn old man. And he must know that his confession would only make it easier for such people, not for himself. In a way, all these questions are unimportant. They come too late. Because the seed of suspicion has been planted. If he is not guilty, however hard he tries, Kundera won't be able to wash himself clean of it. If he is guilty, it is sad, but it doesn't annihilate his writing. If that's any consolation to him,*' she concluded.

A GUIDED TOUR ★

Why am I telling you about this particular case? Because—the way I understand Communism—it still belongs to the Museum. Twenty years after its collapse, it illustrates the state of people's minds here.

My dear Hans, I can hear Milena coming, she'll be back any moment now . . . unfortunately that means you have to go. It was nice of you to visit. I told you, she's not scared of me, even if she is a woman, and we know how hysterical they are about mice. But I'm not sure how she'd react to you—you rats are much bigger. You might scare her. I have to protect her from shock because she has a weak heart. I also have to protect myself—who knows who'll come here if she were to go? I'm sure you understand what I mean.

I hope you found the Museum interesting. I'm afraid that you probably find me not competent enough as a guide. But I couldn't tell how much you know about Communism and I wanted you to get a grasp of it. Remember, I'm only an amateur guide!

[35]

Anyway, Professor Perlik would say, '*What is important is what you do not see—the fear, the complicity and the hypocrisy of life under Communism.*' However modest and superficial the Museum may look to you, the importance of it is that it exists. That, in itself, is a miracle! Because, tell me, who would have ever thought, twenty years ago, that Communism would end up like this—in a *museum*?

Or, for that matter, that you would visit me here, and that I would be your guide?

So long! And have a nice holiday in Paris!

2

An Interview
with the Oldest Dog in Bucharest

So, my dear friend, you've come all the way from Vienna to ask why there are so many dogs on the streets of Bucharest—even at the very centre? You tell me, '*There are an estimated three hundred thousand stray dogs in Bucharest, a city of more than two million people, and there are up to fifty incidents of dogbites per day*'—figures you found in the news.

Striking statistics, and true indeed.

Forgive me for saying so, but you must be a foreigner, here for the first time, to ask about the dogs. I wouldn't call you especially naive. This is what all foreign visitors like you notice first: the impossible traffic situation and the stray dogs. At this time of day, I bet it took you two hours to get from the airport to my home, although it shouldn't have taken more than thirty minutes. Am I right? Of course, but the Romanians are used to it. They prefer to drive their cars, even if they have to drive at the pace of snails. Our local humans don't notice us dogs any longer. If they do, unlike you, they seem not to consider us a problem. You see, with time, one gets used to everything. Even to thousands of dogs in the streets of, shall we say, one of the European Union's capitals.

I agree when you say that we *cani* are cohabitants with humans as long as we don't bite them. I

AN INTERVIEW

also agree when you say that one doesn't see thousands of dogs roaming the streets of, say, Berlin, Paris or, God forbid, Vienna. By the way, I hear that Vienna is a kind of paradise for dogs. Not only are the citizens not bothered by dog droppings (forgive my expression) strewn all over the pavements of that beautiful city, but ladies take them along to fine coffee houses and waiters bring them water. Moreover, they sit in their ladies' laps and eat cakes from small plates of their own—if one can believe *that* kind of rumour. But you're nodding! You've seen it yourself? Oh, it warms my heart that such a place exists in this cruel world! However, not even there do packs of dogs roam free.

I want to say that I understand your curiosity about this subject, my dear friend. It seems that *canine* freedom to move in this city somehow indicates a primitivism in the local humans. Seriously, though, my opinion is that the dog question does not have a simple answer. Maybe I'm too old, maybe you should ask another dog. We dogs are just like you—some of us don't remember, some of us don't care, and, most certainly, we all have different opinions. You happen to be interviewing a very old dog (that is me, Carol, called Charlie) who remembers that the beginning of the whole dog story in Bucharest started during the *ancien régime*, and who happens to think that the displacement of dogs was the consequence of a political decision. In former times, what you habitually call Communism (although there was Communism and 'Communism'), politics used to rule our lives in a more obvious way. I mean both our and our human cohabitants' lives, since our destiny is intertwined.

Without wanting to be pathetic, I can say that we dogs are also victims of the totalitarian regime. I'll tell you why.

But I'm running ahead of myself. I am prone to digressions, you know. It's my age. On the other hand, I was recommended to you precisely because of my age, or rather for my memory, eh? How old am I, you ask? I was born during historic times, in 1990, just before the 'revolution', which makes me extremely old in

AN INTERVIEW ★

dog years. Or roughly 120 in human years. No wonder my mind wanders sometimes . . .

Where was I? Oh yes, we dogs in Romania were victims of Communism. I am afraid that we are no less victims of the post-revolutionary period—as you can see for yourself. My people—or should I say my kind, for the sake of what is nowadays called political correctness?—tell me that life on the streets is getting bloody tough. As if I don't see that myself, just because I don't go out for long walks any more. Ah, my rheumatic legs! But I do see, believe me. Just yesterday I accompanied my friend (you understand, I can't call him Master)—Martin is his name—to the nearby grocery. Mind you, not one of these fancy chain stores—like Billa or Spaar that we have everywhere now—sporting Dutch tomatoes that don't smell or taste of anything. But a small state-owned *Alimentari* that hasn't changed for some reason. Yet. It sells locally grown cabbage heads and half-rotten onions. And there she was, lying in front of the store, an example of our misery for all to see: a beautiful

SLAVENKA DRAKULIC

Labrador bitch, waiting for someone to take pity on her and give her a piece of bread. Waiting, I say, not begging, because you could tell that she was too fine to lower herself to that level. She had sad velvet eyes that reminded me of my mother's.

. . . Anyway, there was another dog on a leash, tied to a fence. Although just an ugly creature and a mixed breed (and I'm not being racist here, merely expressing my indignation), he was looking down upon the Labrador bitch—proud of the status indicated by his leash. A dog on a leash is in possession of something very precious nowadays—a Master. For any dog in Bucharest this is no small matter. It means he's fed regularly, which most dogs aren't. So he looked at the bitch, at her hungry expression, at the infected wound on her ear and her dirty golden coat, and I saw his look. It was full not of empathy but of malice. I was disgusted at his behaviour. Wait here, I told her, and she looked at me with gratitude. My friend Martin gave her a few morsels, he's that kind of person. But that's not a solution for stray dogs. Charity never is a solution for social problems.

AN INTERVIEW ★

You see, here we are, I'm calling for a systematic solution and that, of course, is to slip into politics! Yes, politics about dogs. They too are intelligent creatures. They too need rules.

You tell me you recently visited New English College and that you met a dog there who was mildly curious and decidedly not aggressive. I know him—he was adopted there, lucky sod! But at least he was pleasant. There are many cases of self-adoption or semi-adoption, when people feed the dogs in their neighbourhood and thus domesticate them. As you can imagine, one must adapt or perish. Just think, dogs were the very first animals to be domesticated by humans thousands of years ago. Isn't it a paradox that today humans are doing the same again? However, this isn't the solution either, because, as you know, my lot tend to multiply rather quickly (that's an issue I'll take up a bit later). Suddenly there are too many dogs on the streets and nobody can feed them. As a result, we get hungry—and angry. In other words, by behaving carelessly, we make our own lives harder.

SLAVENKA DRAKULIC

Do you see how this issue is getting more and more complicated?

You've most certainly met the kind of dog that passes you by, looking indifferent or very busy, although I can't think about what. You know, the kind that deliberately avoids eye-contact with you humans. Those wretched creatures are making an effort to maintain their pride, even if—regrettably—they know they live off humans and have always done so. Nowadays, I'm sorry to say, most dogs you meet in the streets of Bucharest bark at you, even try to bite you. As I have already mentioned, the statistics you quoted at the beginning are true. What was that— one of your friends was a victim? One afternoon she was walking home to a rather posh part of town when, all of a sudden, a dog jumped out from under a car and bit her? And she considers herself lucky that it was not a big dog and the wound not serious. Hmm . . . I'd say your friend was indeed fortunate that a solitary dog attacked her. Stray dogs usually operate in packs. She was surely aware of that and therefore did nothing about it, didn't report the incident to, say, the police. What would the police have done? Laughed at her and told her that even they are sometimes attacked. Even today, Romanians rarely report such incidents to the police—or any incidents, for that matter. Who trusts the police?

I'm aware that such attacks—and such stray dogs—would raise alarm in any other city. A mayor would have to come up with a solution. Not here, not in Bucharest. Not even if children are attacked, which happens more often than you might believe. Let me just tell you that, besides organized crime and corruption, organized dog attacks are next! All right, all right, perhaps dogs represent a different kind of danger, but, again, it all depends on how you look at it.

You ask me, how come the same people who got rid of a dictator like Nicolae Ceausescu seem unable to deal with dogs? A legitimate question, indeed, and one I expected. What didn't occur to you is that perhaps people here don't *want* to deal with the dogs. In a way, you see, this whole thing is Ceausescu's legacy, and one of many I might add. How did it all happen? How did he, of all people, let the dogs free? Because, as you say, to imagine he would let anyone free, even if he were a dog, is quite difficult.

See, the street dogs of today are the great-great-grandchildren of the dogs set free in the mid-Eighties, when the old part of central Bucharest was erased from the face of the earth. That is how it all began. And you must be wondering, on the other hand, why a totalitarian regime capable of such destruction, of uprooting tens of thousands of humans, couldn't have taken radical care of its dogs? I suggest you think about something else, about people who obediently abandoned these noble creatures, their best friends (because we're talking here about house pets), to life on the streets, to the cruel struggle of survival. Doesn't that tell you something about those who didn't have the courage to defend their own homes?

Ah, the blessed times when you could blame Ceausescu for everything! At least we dogs weren't responsible for our situation.

AN INTERVIEW

You can tell I'm still bitter about the whole thing. Why? Because of my mother. Mimi was a great lady. We are black poodles with a fine pedigree. However, after that event it didn't matter who was who. Class differences were forsaken and street life imposed another kind of hierarchy. The strongest, not the cleverest, ruled the rest. *Homo homini lupus*, you say to describe such a situation. But I would rather say: *Canis cani homo*!

I hadn't been born when the big eviction happened—it's called resettlement nowadays. But my mother was, and she told me about it. I had the great fortune of living with her in the same household at a tender age (until Martin came along and picked me up) and so I learned my history, which today, regrettably, has been forgotten among my lot—as well as yours, I'd say. These young idiots think it's always been this way, that dogs are born and die in the streets and not, say, in a sixth-floor apartment. They'd have a heart attack if they ever stepped into a lift! Funny, when you think about it, but I've lived almost all my life in such a place. And imagine them, if you can, in the back of the car, going for trip to the seaside! Not that many Romanians had a car, but some did. No, these poor souls think cars are there to hide under from people and the rain. Simple technologies, such as the radio or the TV, are unknown to them. I'd like to know what they'd think of an airplane. I flew in one once—oh, those were the days! I can still taste the biscuit my companion got with his cup of tea and gave to me, naturally. There's something about flying ten thousand metres above the earth, looking through a window at the white clouds and munching on a biscuit.

Sorry, I got carried away again.

Then, before everything went to the dogs, as they say, we dogs were still mostly living with humans, as is the case in every normal country. In their homes and gardens, even in apartment buildings in tiny apartments. Not all of us were in an equal situation, because, to paraphrase George Orwell, a writer I admire, '*we are all equal but some are more equal than others.*' But all of us had a minimum—

AN INTERVIEW

a roof over our heads and a piece of bread, a bite of . . . well, at least *mamaliga*, a kind of polenta, you know. In my long life, I've learned that security is what matters most, both to dogs and to humans. One can witness that now, in this period of total insecurity.

And let me tell you something else—I'm aware I run the risk of being judged pro-Communist, which is foolish—we all worked! It may sound strange to all these unemployed youths on the streets to whom 'work' has no meaning. What do they do? Do they hunt? Do they guard homes and defend them from burglars? Do they announce visitors? Are they employed by the police to chase criminals and sniff out smuggled drugs? Do they lead blind people through the streets of Bucharest? Do they provide love and comfort to their cohabitants? Very few do that today. No, they live in gangs, catch rats, eat rubbish, bite children and beg. Some end up in laboratories as well. The good news for us is that there aren't many scientific experiments going on today in Romania!

SLAVENKA DRAKULIC

Let me go back to Mimi. My mother didn't only witness the eviction from the old quarters, but she herself, together with thousands and thousands, was also a victim of that madness. The orders to destroy the old quarters of downtown Bucharest, like the Uranus neighbourhood where she had lived, came from the court, from Ceausescu himself, as did all orders. Although one could never be sure how much Elena had to do with that grandiose, maniacal plan to build a palace-pyramid called (and I can't help being ironic here) the House of the People. They were both incredibly vain persons and not very intelligent. Perhaps, because of that, they believed they were omnipotent. Tens of thousand of people were evacuated from about eight thousand old buildings and villas into newly built apartments, grey blocks that you can still see standing today. And they were forbidden to take us along. Just when they needed us most to comfort them for their loss, as Mimi used to lament. You see, she was sad for the people, not for her own destiny. That was the kind of person she was. Mimi saw a bulldozer destroying her

AN INTERVIEW ★

beloved family home—its yellow facade, the small garden at the back. It was a horrifying scene—a huge metal hand reaching into the house and pulling out debris, like gutting a fish. Even today, it's hard for me to recall how she described her feeling of helplessness as she watched the destruction. It caused her physical pain, she said. Imagine it—the whole neighbourhood, humans and dogs, standing there and watching, desperate, frightened and powerless . . . without a single voice of protest.

Soon the old houses were gone, even the old scents. Now it smelled of newly dug soil, of cement and bitumen and dogs piss. It was dangerous to go to the building site, but they all did, at first. In disbelief perhaps, as if expecting to wake up from a nightmare. Many dogs died of hunger right away. Without food, vaccination and care, they were quickly decimated. They also died from depression, especially the older dogs. Mimi was young and beautiful and a woman from the outskirts of Bucharest took pity on her. So I was not born on the street. She always reminded me how privileged we were.

★ SLAVENKA DRAKULIC

Anyway, my mother was well connected and had a relative who lived close to the court. He told her that the Ceausescus had two pet dogs. This may surprise you, because you know that both Nicolae and Elena came from a village and that peasants only have working animals, not pets. Besides, Nicolae would never have petted a dog because of his mad fear of bacteria that made him change into a new suit every day. This was a kind of posing, though. Tito of Yugoslavia had two white poodles, not to mention American presidents, the Queen of England and other 'decadent' characters. If it took pet dogs to be considered posh—so be it! Nicolae had a huge black one called Corbu (the Raven), who, they say, had the military rank of Colonel and was driven around in an official car. And our queen, she had a lovely cocker spaniel whose name escapes me now.

No, no, I'm not exaggerating! I know for sure, because once, a very long time ago, our friend Nicu was taking care of some children on vacation in a little house in the mountains close to Ceausescu's villa. One beautiful, sunny, winter's day, the children were out playing in the snow when, all of a sudden, he couldn't hear them any more. There was only the silence. Nicu looked through the window and saw them lying on their backs, perfectly still, a huge black dog standing over them. He rushed out and found the two Ceausescus walking, with the cocker spaniel at their heels and a Securitate officer, very elegant in his military uniform, trailing behind. Nicu happen to be a Dobermann, so he started walking towards Corbu with a murderous look in his eyes. Just then the officer called the dog back. Apparently Corbu was trained to pull to the ground and hover over anything that moved when 'the royal couple' was around. Just remembering that incident would make our, brave cousin shake with rage. So, yes, the Ceausescus were snobbish about the breed of their dogs and 'walked them' now and then.

Nicu, who obviously belonged to a *nomenklatura* family close to the court, also swore he'd witnessed an interesting scene years later. He was present when it was reported to the royal couple that there were

SLAVENKA DRAKULIC

too many dogs roaming free on the streets. Elena laughed. '*Thousands of dogs out on the streets? That's really funny,*' she apparently said. '*Why not kill them all?*' she added, waving her hand and dismissing the whole thing as a big joke. Her husband, meanwhile, didn't even bother to listen. I wonder what Corbu or her own dog thought about those words. I bet they were as arrogant and mean as she was. That's what you humans say about us, that we acquire the character, even the face, of our masters. Although, in the course of my long life, I've also seen the reverse happen.

Interestingly enough, and very unusually so, if I may add, Elena's remark was not taken as a command but as just that, a remark. Someone in the court, either very clever or very cunning, decided that people in Bucharest were shaken enough after being evicted and that it would be dangerous to upset them further by exterminating the dogs. It must have been an experienced courtier who realized that an additional blow like that could shift the delicate balance between the oppressed and the oppressors. The totalitarian power structure resembles a house of cards. You should be very careful when you try to remove a single card, that we all know. But, oddly enough, it's hardest to remove a card from the very top—then it's called a *coup d'état*. That's exactly what happened some years later, right? In other words, there was no need to demonstrate power at that particular moment. Imagine—thousands of dogs lying dead in streets, killed with rat poison, and not enough rubbish trucks and manpower to remove them, the unbearable stink, not to mention the danger of an epidemic. Plus there were all those foreign correspondents to consider: the whole world would have known about Ceausescu's cruelty to animals. It was used to his cruelty to people . . . The Ceausescu regime was a murderous one, but it didn't give its enemies the pleasure of seeing it demonstrated on dogs!

So we lived on.

Well, I also happen to know the story about how the dogs were saved. Yes, there is some advantage in being old, if your brain doesn't turn into

SLAVENKA DRAKULIC

pudding. It was told by a director or manager of a rubbish removal company. Today, he'd be called a CEO, which is a funny title when it's connected with rubbish, you have to admit! One day, Comrade So-and-so was called to a security ministry (everything had to do with security in those days). Naturally, he believed that he had done something wrong. In Ceausescu's Romania, one had to consider such a possibility—the rules were decided by one person alone and were therefore arbitrary. And how! For example, Nicolae was notorious for his indigestion. Therefore, his 'morning decisions', as they were called among his courtiers, were—so to speak—softer than the afternoon or evening ones. It was also rumoured that his cook was instructed to put a small amount of a laxative into his meal if he needed to be mollified before a particularly important decision. Servants have thus played a vital role in our history—if you only think that someone's destiny depended on Ceausescu's indigestion!

So this CEO of the waste disposal company turns up at the ministry, his knees going weak as he

AN INTERVIEW

enters the office of the minister. But the minister, an old friend, hugs him reassuringly. (On the other hand, they would do that even before stabbing you in the back.) Only after a couple of French cognacs (somebody's bribe, he was sure) does our garbage man come to his senses and realize that the minister has really summoned him for a 'consultation'. Since he knows only too well that this could be a ploy to hand over responsibility for a problem, he's not completely relaxed, is he?

Finally, the minister asks him what it would take to clean the city's streets of dogs. The waste disposal man gives the question a quick evaluation. He knows which way the wind blows—but that's not difficult because it always blows from the same direction. The minister's tone indicates that 'cleaning' the city of dogs is not an order (he could have simply said, '*Kill them!*') and thus gives him some room for manoeuvre. '*Well, it would certainly take a lot of work,*' he says, '*plus it wouldn't look* nice.' He's well aware that some decisions in his job are taken according to how nice or not nice the result will appear. Not to people

[59]

inside the country, but to the foreigners, to the enemies, and they are many. '*There was a lot of negative publicity abroad because of the demolition of parts of the old town. Why risk more?*' he adds cautiously. '*Plus, there's a lot of animal-lovers out there who'll go berserk.*'

The minister looks at him without moving a muscle. '*Mikhail,*' he says, feeling secure enough to switch to first names, '*all I'm saying is that it could be done. The dogs could be exterminated. My men—with the help of the army, of course—could gather the carcasses and burn them within a week. But you should be aware that this operation is a sensitive one. It'll all be very, very visible!*' He sees the impact of his words on Mikhail's face, which starts to crease into a grimace that looks faintly like a smile. '*Perhaps it's better to let Nature take its course,*' the minister concludes, thinking of food shortages for the people, never mind the dogs. That old euphemism for starvation causes Mikhail's face to light up. '*Let Nature take its course,*' he repeats excitedly, as if the words were not a banality but divine revelation. The minister hugs Mikhail once more as he leaves, this time cordially. Because, you understand, the minister

AN INTERVIEW ★

couldn't care less for the fate of our canine species. He just wanted the easiest way out for himself.

The CEO was right. The dogs died in silence and no bad publicity was created. Anyway, much more important political issues soon surfaced. Madame Ceausescu had no time to think of dogs, or of anything else for that matter. A couple of years after this incident, her time was up. Truth be told, after they were abducted, an improvised show trial was organized and they were both shot like a couple of old beggars. Ceausescu went down in history as a dictator and most people here think that they both got what they deserved. I would have wanted to see them tried, real and proper. But that wasn't to be. Romanians are foxy people—why complicate things with a trial? Why risk the mad pair saying something nasty about those who executed their orders and who are still alive and kicking, like born-again 'democrats'?

Soon the 'Let Nature take its course' approach took another direction, one unforeseen by our waste disposal man, the minister or anyone else. Living

SLAVENKA DRAKULIC

without any control, the dogs started to multiply. In about two decades, from a mere few thousand we grew to a few *hundred* thousand. The turbulence that society was going through was called a revolution, though it would be more accurate to describe it as a political coup. The best organized forces, such as the Securitate, the police and the military, assumed power. Nobody cared about the dogs.

It was only about a decade later, in 2001 if I remember rightly, that the dogs became the centre of attention. By that time, we really had become visible, and a new, modern generation of Romanians, who barely remembered anything about life under Communism, grew worried about animal rights. Imagine, not human rights but *dog* rights! They pleaded for shelters, medicine, vaccination and sterilization, all the right things, of course. In spite of homeless people, jobless people, hungry people, so many children begging that you could not walk freely, children living in sewage systems not even like dogs but like underdogs . . . Frankly, as much as I was impressed by these dog-lovers, I was puzzled as well. Then a

AN INTERVIEW

certain animal benefactor, a French lady and former famous actress named Brigitte Bardot, who had allegedly been a great sex symbol back in the ancient time of the Sixties, responded to their plea. She still held power over the media. And it was big news. She visited Bucharest, met the mayor and donated money. I still remember how newspapers reported it: '*Ms Bardot has agreed to donate more than one hundred and forty thousand dollars over two years for a mass sterilization and adoption programme for the city's strays, estimated to number three hundred thousand.* [. . .] *For his part, the Mayor of Bucharest, Traian Basescu, has agreed to kill only dangerous, old or terminally ill dogs.* [. . .] *Mr Basescu had earlier insisted that the dogs* [. . .] *must be exterminated.*'

Well, what can I tell you? There was no intention to 'exterminate' the dogs in the first place. Afterwards, that lady's money went to a few shelters, a few sterilizations—you can recognize those dogs by the yellow tags they wear on one ear—and that was that. Most of it just disappeared, as usual.

Listen, I have a nice detail for your story. In the spring of 2008, city authorities cleared all the stray dogs out of the way so that foreign politicians coming to the NATO summit could pass unhindered from the airport to the House of the People, where the summit was held. All the existing shelters were apparently filled with these dogs. You see, typically, our authorities only act when pressured from outside.

It's one of these bittersweet tales, you remark. Bitter, yes, but not sweet. I remember times when Ceausescu's police would clear all 'suspicious elements' of your own species from the streets; now they are down to clearing away the dogs. Strange, very strange.

No doubt this represents progress. This is the twenty-first century, we are in the European Union. Except, all that the Romanians have ever cared about is appearances, not solutions! And I'd say that Romania hasn't changed much in that respect. The 'dog problem' hasn't been solved, if the stray dogs ever really were a problem for the people of Bucharest, which these days I doubt more and more.

AN INTERVIEW ★

You rightly observe that not much was done about the dogs except when foreigners got involved. This, however, brings us to the start of this conversation. You've listened patiently to such a long monologue from an old fool and received no real explanation. But, if you look around, what else can you see besides the stray dogs and the clogged traffic? You see, again, old, beautiful (even if decrepit) villas being demolished to make room for new buildings of steel and glass. For foreign banks and corporations, as in Shanghai or Singapore. For new masters that no longer rule by fear but by greed.

In the transition from Communism to capitalism, all people are unequal but some are more unequal than others.

Stray dogs don't fit into this new capitalist Bucharest, and mayor after mayor promises to do something about it. But he never acts. There are perhaps many reasons for not acting and, moreover, for not knowing how to act. One could certainly blame it on cowboy capitalism, corrupt bureaucracy, bad politics or disappointment with the EU. But I happen to believe that, in Romania, dogs are considered the victims both of Communism and of the democratization process (or the transition period, as they call it) as much as are your own kind. I observe that an individual in this society feels pretty lost and helpless. He doesn't know how to take responsibility for his own life, much less for that of the poor dogs in his neighbourhood.

It doesn't help that democracy has so far meant that only those who are up stay up. It also could be a *laissez-faire* attitude of this society in general, which hasn't woken up properly from its Communist slumber. Generally speaking, people still believe that there will always be someone 'up there' to take a decision in their names whom they can blame later on. If yesterday it was Communism, today it's the bureaucracy in Brussels. Leaving everything to the higher-ups, not taking the initiative, not willingly acting in the common interest—this, in my modest dog opinion, is really what our problem is. What to do *when there's not even an idea of a common interest, a common good?* In a society like ours, it needs to be created. The lack of it means that, one day, we'll wake up to a decision taken by someone high up that '*the dogs have to go.*' In the name of the EU, we'll be swept away for good. Then there will be a short outrage, the party in charge will perhaps lose a few votes. So what?—one may think. But permit me to ask these harsh questions: who will be next? Gypsies, perhaps? Or Jews? Why not people with glasses?

Sorry, sorry. As I said, I tend to get carried away. Look at me, an old dog delivering speeches! As you can see, in Romania even dogs are political animals.

You could almost take this whole canine story as a metaphor for humans in Romania: victimized, abandoned, poor, hungry for everything, totally disillusioned. But this would be a bad metaphor because, unlike humans, the dogs won't get together and vote for someone like Napoleon (I'm referring to *Animal Farm*, George Orwell's ingenious parable) or start a war. And here I'd like to leave you, my friend, to ponder over frustrations that lead to populism—

SLAVENKA DRAKULIC

and to wait and see what these newly declassed masses will come up with, who will manipulate them and how.

But before we part, let me tell you just one more story, this time a different one. Have you heard of the 'Baghdad Pups'? No? Of course not, this is a typical American venture. It's about stray dogs in Afghanistan and in Iraq and about the American soldiers who befriended them. The boys want to take their friends back home with them to the US, but it proves to be against the law. However, a certain navy lieutenant was so in love with his Cinnamon (what an idiotic name for a dog, I must say!) that he managed to do the impossible. He gave Cinnamon to a contractor who took him to Bishkek in Kyrgyzstan. But the man could not put the dog on a civilian flight to the US, so he abandoned Cinnamon at the airport. An airline employee gave the pup to a local family. Then the lieutenant's energetic sister stepped in and, with the help of some organization or other, located the lost dog. Now Cinnamon lives happily ever after in Maryland. Americans being Americans,

AN INTERVIEW

they immediately realized that there are more soldiers who would like to do the same, so they organized 'Operation Baghdad Pups'. Their newspapers report that so far more than thirty pet stray dogs have been brought over—don't ask me how! The point is that Americans do things by themselves. They don't wait and despair.

Now, what shocked me are the costs of such rescue trips, between four thousand and six thousand dollars per dog. That gave me an idea. True, unfortunately Romania is not occupied by American soldiers. But why shouldn't we take action ourselves and, under the slogan *Export, not extermination* (I imagine this could catch media attention), offer our dogs for adoption? I'm sure that there are people willing to take them; the costs would be one third of the American, if not less. Remember how the Westerners were crazy about adopting our children from orphanages? Not that dogs are as popular as white orphans, but one could at least try. For example, what if adoption included a free, long weekend in Bucharest with your future pet? Of course, someone is bound to label this *dog tourism* but I think it is better and more decent than, for example, sex tourism. The more I think about the idea, the more I like it. But being an old and experienced dog, I suspect that the Romanians would rather do real business by selling dogs to the Koreans as meat! In fact, I'm surprised that no one has had that idea. (I've heard rumours about something like that in Budapest's China Town.) The state would probably subsidize it and some smart-ass with good connections would get rich over our dead bodies. And then he'd launch himself head-on into politics, including in his programme the defence of animal rights! Nothing would surprise me.

But what's that you say? I see your face—you're smiling and shrugging your shoulders. You must think I'm mad.

Hey, relax, after all I'm only a dog!

3
The Cat-Keeper in Warsaw
(A Letter to the Prosecutor)

Dear Mr Prosecutor,

I am writing to your office and to you as the person in charge of case No. PT/2875/2008–09, regarding the defendant, whom, for reasons of my own, I will here refer to only as 'the General'. As you are

SLAVENKA DRAKULIC

well aware, in the autumn of 2008, the Institute of National Remembrance, investigating Nazi and Communist era crimes, brought in an indictment against a total of nine persons. The eighty-six-year-old General, who headed the Military National Salvation Council, created on 13 December 1981, now stands accused, among other things, of leading this 'criminal organization'—for which he could get up to ten years in prison.

I will abstain from any comment about this Institute and its methods in conducting the *lustration* process—perhaps it is enough to mention that I have heard some humans call it the 'Ministry of Truth'. But, on the other hand, I do not go out in the streets of Warsaw very often and it could be that I am missing some valuable information.

I am appealing to you because I believe it is extremely important to bring the case of the General urgently to an end. I will try to explain why.

You may rightly ask, who am I to take it upon myself to address you at all? Therefore, please allow

THE CAT-KEEPER ★

me first to introduce myself. My name is Gorby. I am a female of feline origin—what you humans call a cat. Born in the house of the General's daughter, I have been living in the General's household for almost ten years now. His whole family loves animals; the General himself, unfortunately, favours horses the most. No wonder. He is an officer after all. Let me explain our relationship. I am considered the General's pussycat, although I take a somewhat different view of this myself. It is I who is kind enough to choose to live in his home, and to allow him and everybody else to believe just the opposite. It is perhaps too banal to say that I picked him up, since it is well known that we cats are free spirits, unlike dogs. But I have to share the house with his dog Napoleon. This is because Napoleon Bonaparte is the person the General most admires. Not a good choice of name, because Napoleon is a large dumb mongrel. The only certain thing about his lineage is that he evidently belongs to the lower end of a gene pool. Of course, his favourite pastime is to play with a ball! The poor thing shows no sign of intellectual

★ SLAVENKA DRAKULIC

activity whatsoever, and I can tell that he bores the General. Who wouldn't be bored by throwing about that round object again and again? But I have some use of him—he brings me news and information from the outside world. A sort of courier, you might say.

I, on the other hand, am neither bored nor boring. *'You're arrogant,'* I've heard Napoleon say about me more than once behind my back, but it is not my intention here to gossip about him. I merely want to stress the fact that it was my *choice* to live with the General. *To choose* is a very important verb for me. I have no problem with freedom, since I did not live in that allegedly *inhuman* period of human history called Communism. I have often heard this adjective—by *inhuman* humans mean *animal-like*. Let me take a chance here to express my total disagreement with this use of the word. It should be corrected! Needless to say, we animals rarely exercise your bloody habit of killing each other within the same species. With the exception of fighting dogs—but those gladiators are beneath contempt, I'm afraid.

THE CAT-KEEPER ★

Going back to my relationship with the General. I cannot say that he is my butler, although it is very close to the truth. It would offend him were I to claim thus. The General is very much a person of the old days. By that I mean that he is truly sensitive to class differences, maybe even more so because he was born into a noble family. *Noblesse oblige*! So, let us simplify things and state here that the General is my keeper.

With this introduction, I would like to move to the purpose of my letter and offer you some of my reflections.

I have two reasons for submitting this appeal to you. The first is strictly personal. At this moment, the General is in hospital with a severe case of pneumonia and various other ailments that I will not now bother you with. This is not the first time. His age and the stress of this trial are wearing him out. Pneumonia can cause the death of an old and frail person. Considering his poor health all his life, I am seriously worried that he may not make it to hear the sentence. Especially because, in this country, such trials can drag on for years. Quite some time has elapsed from the first indictment to the beginning of his trial . . . I would hereby like, as his friend—indeed his *confidant*—to submit this appeal to you to take matters into your own hands and bring a quick decision in whatever direction you see fit.

My second reason is of a more general nature. I see the young generation of Poles: for them, Communism is something that died twenty years ago, before they were even born. It is passé! Although this young generation may not be very knowledgeable about, or even interested in, the events of the past, they should be responsible for how they deal with their past *now*. Therefore, the trial of the General is a very important example for them.

Speaking of the General, I ask myself if he (and others from his time) should have been put on trial at all? And what is such a trial expected to achieve? To clarify my point, I do think that a fair trial makes it possible for a person unjustly accused to exonerate himself. I also wonder if the General should have

THE CAT-KEEPER

been put on trial in a criminal court. After all, he is not a war criminal. Let's make no mistake here— the General welcomes his trial: '*It is important that history doesn't continue to divide Poles for ever,*' he has told me often enough. I believe that the decision to try him or not was a major dilemma, because it had to do with the attitude of your society towards the Communist past in general. Lacking a general consensus on how to proceed, your office dragged its feet until very recently. After all, life is what happens precisely in between these (or any other) two extremes. Again, as the General himself said, '*History and the question of who is right are complicated and cannot be seen in terms of black and white.*'

I am sure that you, with your experience in such matters, will agree with me about truth and justice being brother and sister—but sometimes it is hard to maintain an equilibrium without causing even more harm to society. After all, a courtroom should not deal with moral issues but with individual guilt proved by evidence. The important question in the

★ SLAVENKA DRAKULIC

General's case is: what values do you want to promote—retaliation or social consensus, further conflict or reconciliation? That is my understanding, although Napoleon claims that this trial has nothing to do with either truth or justice—only politics. Well, perhaps he overheard somebody saying this, for I cannot imagine he deduced it on his own . . .

The General is, as they say in the media, a *divisive figure* in Polish society. There is no doubt about the controversy he has been provoking for almost two decades now, long before I was even born. (Please note, Mr Prosecutor, that I am being very honest with you, to the point of even admitting my age, which a cat-lady should never do!) So the controversy, which everybody knows about by now, is that the General claims he declared martial law in order to save Poland from Soviet invasion. In short, he saved lives through an act of patriotism. For twenty years, the General has been consistently defending his decision: '. . . *we were threatened with fratricidal conflict, and we could have inflicted on ourselves incalculable tragedy.*'

THE CAT-KEEPER ★

Today, in spite of this controversy, the General's public standing is better than the Kaczynski brothers'! For years, opinion polls—about whether or not the Poles believe his justification for martial law—have been roughly split down the middle. That suggests that at least one half of Poland's citizens accept it. And they do not think it necessary to put the General on trial. After all, most Poles did not choose to live under Communism; they merely went along with it, accepting the military regime as reality. It is not in their interest to go back to the past and wash their own dirty linen. The other half, however, would like to 'purify' society of its Communist remnants. They prefer a fresh start, a sharp division between past and present, between totalitarianism and democracy. For such purists, Poland was divided into Communist supporters and the opposition, with nothing in-between. To them, the trial of the General represents an act of revenge. '*A traitor is not a victim of circumstances*,' they say. But this is a moral statement and is not helpful to the trial. I would hesitate to disregard the possibility that the General was acting out of patriotism—but I may be prejudiced about him. Because, I ask myself, does the fact that he was a Communist rule out his patriotism? I think not.

'*Down with the enemy!*' barks Napoleon incongruously when I—out of sheer pity—tell him about the pros and cons of the trial. Sometimes, as an intellectual, I feel a responsibility to keep him informed. But what can such a poor creature think, when I ask him '*Who is the enemy?*' except that I am showing off?

The truth about the General is that he did indeed proclaim martial law on 13 December 1981. The truth is that, as a consequence, the Solidarity movement was banned, its members were persecuted and jailed, censorship was introduced, freedom suspended and fifty-six people killed in the year that followed—that is all true. The General does not dispute any of this. On the contrary, he has publicly expressed his regret. The truth is also that, in his

THE CAT-KEEPER ★

political career, he made other wrong decisions, inflicting pain on the Poles. Even when he was not acting on his own, but as a member of the ruling political elite, for example while dispatching Polish troops to Prague in 1968 as part of the Warsaw Pact invasion. Or when there was the shooting in Gdansk in 1970 in which forty-four protesters were killed. The truth is that he was a political leader who had accumulated too many functions (Prime Minister, Minister of Defence, President, Head of the Military Council of National Salvation), logically leading him to assume dictatorial power.

I understand all this. Perhaps this is the moment to stress again that I am sentimental, that I would like to defend the General. However, while I am on his side in my heart, I try to keep a clear head: I don't want to defend him from the truth—blind faith is his dog's defining trait, not mine.

Before I take you any further, you should bear in mind my special position. I have a chance to observe the General from a very privileged perspective, being the one that sits in his lap most often. Napoleon is too big. And, thank God, we don't yet keep horses in the house, except as pictures. So, he caresses me. He speaks to me. He trusts me, I would say. You see, I am small and elegant and I try not to be obtrusive. Sometimes I purr, just to make him feel good. Usually, I sit there quietly. I watch and I listen. Like any 'real' psychiatrist.

He is bony, and his lap is not very comfortable to say the least. But he is warm, and that counts for a lot when you are not so young yourself. And he strokes me, which I've found out is good for my back. He does it somewhat absentmindedly because he does it while he reads, and he reads a lot, or listens to the news on the radio—he hardly ever watches TV—in his small studio on the first floor of the house. I let him do it, I mean rub me and read at the same time. You can't take away all the fun from an old man, now can you? It wouldn't be nice of me. Meanwhile, I ponder on subjects of my interest . . .

My real interest is not politics but psychology. Being, well, a semi-professional, I don't judge people.

THE CAT-KEEPER ⭐

You may think I need to study the psyche of the General because I depend upon his will. Or because I need to know my enemy. I would not go that far; the General is a good cat-keeper. He does not taunt me with bizarre, little dangling objects, as other humans do. I get far better treatment than Napoleon, who is extremely jealous of my privileged position, grumbling stupidly that it isn't fair. As if life were fair! In return, I listen and try to understand the General. I also try to understand humans as such, with their strengths and weaknesses. I am, on the whole, fond of your kind of primate! I find you as a species interesting, often puzzling, mostly not very intelligent—but worth observing. You perhaps do not fully trust the opinions of a feline psychiatrist without adequate formal education? But please consider that I am in a position to closely scrutinize how human beings behave—*I do nothing but observe them full time.*

Now, I am well aware that you may harbour a certain suspicion that I am subjective, i.e. prejudiced in favour of my keeper. But let me assure you that my subjective feelings do not stand in the way of my professional findings about the said human being. On the contrary, I treat him like any other patient of mine, like, for example, his wife (a very nice lady, loved by her students!) and his darling daughter. The pet daughter! Yet, there is no competition between the two us—she has far too little time and patience for the old man . . . No, I am certainly able to keep the necessary distance between the object of my study and myself. In fact, the General does not even know that I am writing this letter. I had to do it in secret because he would strongly disapprove, perhaps even scold me if he found out. I only worry that Napoleon, in his simplicity, may let slip something to him. But he barks pretty incomprehensibly and the General is a bit deaf—so perhaps I have nothing to worry about after all.

Mr Prosecutor, allow me to make a digression. I am afraid I have to use this opportunity to make you aware of an injustice in your domain. I am convinced that I qualify as a character witness at the

THE CAT-KEEPER

General's trial. I personally volunteered to tell the court that he is a good man. I have sent enough obvious signs of my intention. I also sent a letter to the judge. Believe it or not, I was rejected from testifying on the grounds of my—species! A judge of the criminal court rejected me as a character witness with the following words: '*We hereby inform you that, as a rule, our court does not accept witnesses of alien origin.*' First and foremost, I am not an alien. *ET is an alien*— I am a cat! Disregarding this display of ignorance on the part of the said judge, where does your law make this stipulation? He did not even bother to cite the clause that forbade such witnesses, a grave mistake for someone who is responsible for the law.

I ask you now: who is really harbouring prejudices here, not to use the word discrimination or even racism for the view expressed by the judge? Should I have responded by demonstrating exactly the same kind of prejudice towards your own species and observed that he was only a *primate*!? I do have my feline pride, you know! If this judge of yours

SLAVENKA DRAKULIC

were a true Polish gentleman in the first place, he would never have allowed himself to offend a lady.

But let us put this distasteful issue aside. After all, I am not the subject of this letter. I feel that it is my duty to tell you more about the General. So let me tell you now, if I may, about the crucial moment in the General's life, about the moment of his decision of December 1981.

'*Listen, Gorby,*' he told me one evening in that agitated mood that sometimes overcomes him. '*People should believe me that there was no other way. I had no choice in December 1981. It really was a matter of the lesser evil, as is often the case in politics. You, of all creatures, know how rarely I speak about that part of my life . . . I do not like to remember those moments—you call it repression, no? Oh, if only you had been there in Moscow that December night when the Soviet comrades summoned me to a meeting of the Politburo, for "consultations". I still remember the tense air in the room. Leonid Brezhnev was sitting at the head of a long table with his bulldog face and beady eyes. He was already very ill, but no less dangerous for that. And Andropov, breathing down his neck.*

THE CAT-KEEPER ★

These comrades looked to me like a pack of dangerous dogs, ready to bite. Not much was said, but from their looks I understood the precarious situation Poland was in, with the Solidarity movement's demands undermining the entire Communist system. They were afraid that the "Polish pestilence"—as one of them put it—would spread if it was not "contained". That reminded me of 1968, when we in Poland were forced to send our soldiers against our brothers in Prague. How I regret that today! And how sadly it ended there, how we crushed Dubcek and his reforms!

It should have been clear to me then what was clear to Brezhnev in 1981—that Communism was not a system that could be reformed and that any such attempt would only bring it down. Gorbachev did not understand that either, unbelievable as it sounds. When, almost two decades later, it was Gorbachev's turn to try reform, how did it end? With the collapse of almost the entire Communist world. I admire that man for his brave attempt to do the impossible—but I do not understand why he didn't learn from the failure of the "Prague Spring" and from martial law in Poland. Was he so naive? Or just a hard-core believer in Communism, like me?

★ SLAVENKA DRAKULIC

Anyway, in 1981, Brezhnev was not naive at all. He forced me to act, because he knew what we did not. There was no question of the Soviets leaving us in peace to slowly reform our Communism as we saw fit. They did not want another Alexander Dubcek. As Brezhnev-the-bulldog told me in no uncertain terms before the meeting with the others: "How long do you intend to tolerate anarchy? Either you take care of your problems, or we will." *His words were not open to interpretation, my friend. He did not suggest that, for example, I should resign if I didn't curb the protests—nothing as benign as that. That would have been an easy choice. I would have gladly done it. True, he never said what his threat really meant, he never mentioned the words* military intervention—*in that my opponents are right. The Soviet threat was never spelled out! But there was not the slightest doubt as to what Brezhnev and all the rest really had in mind.*

You may wonder if I was afraid. Later, people asked me if I felt physically threatened. I fought in the Second World War, Gorby. I know what fear is. No, this was not the fear of death that one feels in war. All soldiers feel it, it's only human. But when you are fighting, there is a certain moment when fear turns into indifference. Or into a reconciliation with

THE CAT-KEEPER ⭐

ones destiny, an acceptance of the consequences. You cannot fight and be afraid all the time. Therefore, you have to make peace with yourself—perhaps not consciously. I believe it is the survival instinct that makes us acknowledge death in order to live. What a beautiful contradiction, when you think of it!

I remember I went to the men's room. There was a mirror there. I looked at myself. I felt calm, just like in 1943 when I was sure I would be killed by the Germans in battle. So, then and there, in the toilet of the Kremlin palace, I made my decision—Poland would be saved from invasion! I was ready to sacrifice my reputation rather than the lives of my people. Let me make this clear to you—I was well aware of the price I would have to pay for such a decision and, as my mother would say, I was ready to bear my cross. But, back then, I thought that, one day, when the crisis of Communism was over (imagine, how trusting I was!), my people would realize that my decision had been necessary in order to save their lives. Back in the conference room, I told our Soviet comrades that they need not worry, we Poles would take care of our "problems" ourselves. I could not, of course, repeat the word "pestilence". Brezhnev stood up, slapped me on the back and grinned unpleasantly. That was it.'

★ SLAVENKA DRAKULIC

This is what the General himself confessed to me. Therefore the problem of this trial, as I see it now, is that it will be his word against those who say that there was no Soviet invasion planned. Indeed, of late, it is alleged that some documents have been found in support of this. But who could have known that then?

To all this I could add a few conclusions about his character: the General is a serious person. You rarely see a photo of him smiling, only in family photos perhaps. Usually he is sombre, his dark glasses adding to his gloom, showing that he carries a heavy weight on his shoulders. Although he is not without a sense of humour! He is a man of principles, even if these principles are different from yours or mine. As an illustration, I will only tell you that he did not enter the church at the funeral of his mother, an ardent Catholic. No, not even in plain clothes. He waited outside until the service was over. '*A Communist army General does not go to church under any circumstances*!' he told me later. Even if you don't believe me, I can vouch that for him duty is above all else. This—permit me to say—is not a very Catholic value. Besides, he proved to be intelligent and capable of grasping the new situation and adapting to it. A complex personality . . . Which is precisely my reason for writing this letter, in my capacity as both a specialist in human psychology and his friend. Do I even need to tell you that Napoleon, when I told him about my intention of writing this letter, dismissed it sneeringly, calling you '*a bloodsucker*'?—but that is his level, I am afraid.

In spite of his—not my!—low opinion of you, I would like to trust you. I have already said that my name is Gorby, after Gorbachev. I am well aware that you—like many others before you—may be puzzled by that. The General himself chose it, although, considering my female gender, it would have been more appropriate, wouldn't it, to have named me Raisa, after Gorby's wife whom he loved so dearly. It seems like a paradoxical twist that the General (my pet human) should name his pet cat after somebody who dismantled Communism and, therefore, should be his enemy. But, believe me, he had

★ SLAVENKA DRAKULIC

his reasons. He admired Gorby—almost like Napoleon (the man, not the dog, of course). The mere fact that he named me after Gorby should tell you a lot about the General himself.

The great absurdity of Gorby's life was that *the collapse of Communism was the result of his own attempt to reform it*, to perfect it, as he himself said. Isn't that a sad destiny, to live to see exactly the opposite of what you intended? To have the whole world admire you for something that you did not want to achieve? To see people applaud you for the mistake you made? In hindsight, it looks like a comedy, but it is a tragedy! So, *they both believed in the possibility of saving Communism*, one way or another, and they both ended up losers. Gorby is almost like a character from a comedy of errors. Think about it—the outstanding political change of the twentieth century happened, in fact, by mistake!

Gorby was, no doubt, a believer. The General was a believer, too. '*A faith is not acquired by reasoning . . . Reason may defend an act of faith but only after the act*

THE CAT-KEEPER

has been committed, and the man committed to the act,' wrote Arthur Koestler. I think that, for the General—as for many other believers—the main problem was the difference between theory and practice: obviously, for him, in theory, Communism looks good. So, let us suppose, for the sake of argument, that you are a true Communist (you have acquired a faith) who, early enough, becomes aware of the 'deviations' in practice. You are part of the power structure. You think you can do better. What do you do? You reach for, shall we say, unethical means in order to achieve your aim. You act brutally in order to save your beloved Poland from the invasion, in accordance with the principle of the end justifying the means. That is, you make a pact with the devil, in this case, Moscow. But—and this is not an excuse, only a clarification—you act as a man of faith. Later, you understand the consequences of what you have done and you regret your decision—only it is too late. Can you be redeemed? Do you deserve pity? Well, that depends upon the circumstances, I suppose you would say.

★ SLAVENKA DRAKULIC

In both my feline—that is, subjective—and professional view, the General is perhaps an even more tragic person than Gorbachev. He lost the battle to improve Communism by ruthless means and *destroyed his moral credibility*, which was not the case with Gorbachev. The General is tragic for another reason—because he has publicly admitted that he was defeated. He claims he believes Communism failed, that he is now a social democrat and, moreover, that he likes Poland as it is today. Yet *he has never repented for martial law*! He has never admitted that his decision to impose it had been wrong. On the contrary, he still maintains that it was a necessary measure to save Poland . . . In other words, the General did not do the single most important thing that would have saved him from being put on trial—he did not repent. And that is unforgivable—at least for half of the Polish citizens. He is not to be forgiven for standing up for his belief. He has to pay for his sins!

This attitude, in a time of moral decay is, you have to admit, rather brave, I'd say.

THE CAT-KEEPER

Napoleon 'comments' about your kind of justice in just a few words—'*an eye for an eye*'. Being a cat, I do not trust dogs, and I cannot believe in such primitivism on the part of democratic Poland. Please! I am aware of how pathetic I may sound now, but the General must be given a chance to redeem himself. In your religion, everyone must be given a chance. You must have considered whether there is something to say in his defense. Correct me if I am wrong, but it was the General who made possible the first free elections which Solidarity won. You could claim that, in a way, he was forced to the round-table talks in the spring of 1989—or to invite Solidarity to enter the coalition government. He also stepped down from the Presidency. He considers Solidarity's later triumph to have been made possible by the decisions he took during and after the imposition of martial law.

However, something like a Solidarity-generation complex still runs very deep in this society. I mean that participants in the round-table negotiations with

SLAVENKA DRAKULIC

the General are themselves being treated as traitors. Politics is the art of compromise and compromise (enabled by the General) brought about the change of power. Yet, political compromise, dialogue and consensus—even if they played a great role in the Nineties—are not sufficiently part of this culture. This is not hard to understand in view of the past: what could you humans learn about compromise when you were living in a totalitarian society? But this complicates the case of the General even more . . .

I know, Mr Prosecutor, that justice is needed, but, I ask you: what is justice in the case of the General? Going back to where I started: does he really have to be tried in a criminal court like an ordinary criminal or Mafioso? Are you sure this trial will satisfy the principle of justice? Some authorities in the field of law, for example, have expressed their doubts that the charges stand. Is the trial going to be useful, or perhaps harmful, to society? The General himself is not opposing a trial, because it gives him yet another chance to say what he considers to be the truth. He cares about his role in history and he wants to set the record straight.

Napoleon, predictably, unquestioningly believes every word of the General. He is, you know, very much the soldier type. I, on the other hand, think that my duty as a feline intellectual is to ask the right questions. The main question is: what is the purpose of this trial? Is it to achieve symbolic justice, or is it a case of belated retribution? Is he being tried as a person or as a symbol? Formally, he was put on trial for illegally imposing martial law. It is expected to be a ritual exorcizing of the evil spirit of Communism and, as such, to help society mentally step out of its past. In that sense, perhaps it will be wise to hold a trial. But if you are honest, you must admit that, so far, this looks like an act of revenge for decades of Communist rule—no more and no less. Vengeance, however, is a bad motive. Your office should not take part in something like that. What will you achieve? Are you sure that you are not looking for a scapegoat, not knowing how to deal with the problematic past?

Besides, it should be taken into consideration that the General has expressed regret for the pain his decision has brought to many of his fellow humans. I do not need to remind you, of all people, that only a person with an ethical code could do so. This is no small matter. '*I am sorry. I regret mainly the social costs of this dramatically difficult decision and those cases where particular people suffered*,' he said. A man needs to be a strong character to be able to say this, you have to give him that!

I am not asking the victims to forgive the General. I merely believe that it is important for a society to be able to demonstrate mercy. Polish society is as tolerant and wise as the mercy it can bestow upon humans like the General. Why am I calling for mercy? Because, in my opinion, it would be important for this society to realize that the General was defeated long ago—and one does not flog a dead horse. In his case, would it not be better to demonstrate some benevolence and let him continue to live in moral condemnation instead? Politically, he has already been a loser for twenty years now. Leave the final sentence to history. In doing so, you will show the compassionate side of the Polish government and society in whose name you act. I remember what Adam Michnik, the dissident imprisoned under the General, with whom I tend to agree, once said about the whole affair of the trial: '*It's a subject for historians, writers, priests, moralists and confessors—not for the courts.*'

On the other hand (because there is always the other side to consider in such matters), there is an argument that holds that the tribunal at Nuremberg did more to pass a verdict on Nazism than generations of historians . . .

But there is something else that worries me. To prosecute the General in a criminal court is simply an act of humiliation. By humiliating the General, the Poles will also be humiliating themselves. They will be spitting on forty-five years of their own past, their own lives—like two people after a bitter divorce. Perhaps that is one of the reasons why so many Poles accept his justification of martial law as a 'lesser evil'? The others, who insist on his trial,

SLAVENKA DRAKULIC

however, perhaps believe that all *their* sins would be redeemed once sentence was passed—as if the General were Jesus. Does this sound like a metaphor to you? A literary gimmick of mine? Well, I love literature, but that is not the case here. No, in the case of the General, *redemption is the cultural matrix* we are looking at in this society, Catholic to the core. Redemption of their Communist sins will come in very handy, because it will rid them of their own responsibility. Is the General the only one to blame for martial law? No, there were thousands and hundreds of thousands who aided and abetted military rule for more than a decade. What about them? Not every Pole was a member of the Solidarity movement. Once the General is sentenced, the others can wash their hands.

In saying all this, what am I actually proposing you do?

First and foremost, I ask you to make your decision quickly, whatever it may be. I am not suggesting you suspend the trial, although clearly I

THE CAT-KEEPER

would prefer that solution as the wisest. I think I have presented my arguments for that option, but you may find them inadequate and decide for the trial to go on. If so, please do so, but order the court to move quickly. The General is an old and frail man. If you do not hurry, he has no chance of seeing the end of it. It is my worst nightmare that he will die before the trial is over. Of course I will be devastated by his passing—I am his pet, after all. But his death will present society with another problem: if you allow it to happen, there will be no closure. And that is what is expected of his trial, to close the chapter on Communism. You know what happened with the Slobodan Milosevic case in The Hague? Not that I compare the two; in my opinion there is no comparison between the General—a tragic believer in Communism who made a pact with the devil in good faith—and an opportunistic manipulator, a thug and a war criminal. Milosevic died long before his trial was over. And, because of that, the Serbs were never confronted with their responsibility for the wars in the Balkans. Denial rules in

SLAVENKA DRAKULIC

Serbia today. As if he and his murderous nationalist politics were never on trial. No truth, no justice, no closure or catharsis . . . nothing.

For the sake of Poland, I would like you to avoid this happening here! Your responsibility is great and I urge you to be aware of it. Even Napoleon agrees with me on this, although I am not sure that he understands the problem at all.

With this appeal, I salute you in the hope that you will not disregard my letter just because I was fortunate enough to be born a cat, and not a human being.